Winnie~the~Pooh
Goes to
London

EGMONT

You could tell that Christopher Robin had something important to say from the way he clasped his knees tightly and wriggled his toes. Everybody gathered round and looked at him expectantly.

'Her Majesty ...' Christopher Robin began.

'Oh,' squeaked Piglet in a state of great excitement.

'Her Royal Highness ...' he went on.

'Quite so, quite so,' agreed Rabbit.

'The Queen of England ...' he said quickly before anyone else could interrupt him.

'Oh, the Queen,' said Pooh Bear, much relieved. 'The other people you mentioned sounded much too tall and fearsome, but the Queen is quite different.'

Pooh had once sent a letter and was told to stick on a small picture of the Queen. It stuck more to his nose than to the letter but it told the postman that it was Most Urgent and that The Queen Says It Must Be Sent and so he was sure it had been.

'As I was saying,' said Christopher Robin, passing Pooh a honey sandwich so that he might continue speaking, 'Her Majesty the Queen lives in a very great city, called London. I would very much like to go there and perhaps I might have tea with the Queen.'

'If you go to London,' said Rabbit, importantly, 'you must take the Queen a present. Something she will treasure.'

'I've never had much luck finding treasure,' sighed Pooh. 'But I did once find the North Pole. Do you suppose the Queen might like that?'

The friends thought this an excellent idea but it wasn't long before they realised that finding the North Pole once was a very fine thing but that finding it again was an altogether different thing.

Suddenly the Forest seemed to be full of sticks that could or could not be the North Pole.

'This will never do,' announced Rabbit.

'Do ...' mumbled Pooh. 'That brings to mind a little hum which I'd like to hum if it was felt that a hum was called for at such a time of thoughtfulness.' And without waiting for a reply he began:

The Queen lived in her palace, as Queens often do.
Doing all those busy things that busy Queens do.
But the Queen could never know, as you and I do,
That doing nothing much can be the BEST thing to do.

So from a forest far away, on this sunny day,
We're sending you some quiet and a little time to play.

And quiet there was. The sort of quiet that makes the tip of your nose turn a sunset-shade of pink.

'Bear,' announced Christopher Robin solemnly. 'That hum is fit for a Queen. Owl shall write it out and you and I and Eeyore will deliver it to Buckingham Palace. And Piglet must come too because London is a very big place indeed and even small animals, if they are very good friends, can make everything alright.'

Christopher Robin also found a beautiful, bright red balloon for Piglet to hold.

'That way we won't lose you in the crowd,' he said.

Piglet held on very tightly to the balloon. He wasn't quite sure what a crowd was, something like a dark cloud perhaps, but in any case he didn't want to get lost in it and was pleased the balloon would help.

So, the present was ready and, side-by-side, Winnie-the-Pooh (Edward Bear, Bear of Very Little Brain, Brave Adventurer and Loyal Friend), his small companion Piglet, Eeyore and Christopher Robin set off for London.

'Of course, London is on quite the other side,' remarked Christopher Robin as they were walking.

'Of the sea?' asked Pooh, somewhat alarmed.

'Not the sea, I shouldn't think,' replied Christopher Robin, whose geography lessons so far had been mostly spent colouring in edgy bits. 'But certainly the country or county. I'm not quite sure which. In any case, it is very far off and we shall have to catch a train.'

'I do hope it wants to be caught,' said Pooh, who was already a little out of puff from the walk.

But the train was good enough to stop for them in the station so there was no catching to be done at all and there was plenty of time to climb aboard and find four comfy seats and then they were off!

'Would you be so kind as to stay very close by?' asked an anxious Piglet as they got off the train at Victoria Station. He hadn't expected London to have quite so many legs.

There were pinstriped legs, big-booted legs and some legs balanced on pointy shoes, which seemed to have a little stick stuck to the bottom of each sole. And they were all in a terrible rush and seemed to know exactly where they were going.

Christopher Robin, Pooh, Piglet and Eeyore launched themselves into this vast forest of legs and hoped they'd come out alright.

They emerged into a busy street. Christopher Robin told them that the large, black vehicles rushing past were called Traffic.

Pooh thought that Traffic looked like giant, shiny beetles and thinking of them as beetles made it less worrying.

The friends walked and they walked. But Eeyore's sighs, that had started out as small puffs, were now growing so large and loud that they were worried he would run out of puff altogether, and Winnie-the-Pooh's legs were known for their stoutness, not their brisk walking and Piglet's legs were so short that they were hardly worth speaking of at all, so Christopher Robin suggested they ride on a bus to see more of London.

'Most considerate, I'm sure,' sighed Eeyore, although slightly less puffily this time.

The friends had never been on a bus before and this was a most unusual one. It had winding stairs and up at the top there was no roof at all. As the bus began to move the wind did its best to blow Piglet's ears right off.

'We'll call this the Blustery Bus,' laughed Christopher Robin.

The bus took the friends past a great many important buildings and Christopher Robin didn't know all the names. There was one very grand old shop which Pooh found strangely familiar but he told himself he was being silly as this was surely his first visit to London.

At the next stop they were able to get out and stretch their legs a little.

'Look at that tree, Pooh,' gasped Piglet as they stepped off the bus. And what an extraordinary tree it was. Taller than even the Bee Tree in the Hundred Acre Wood and much less woody. In fact it wasn't woody at all.

It reminded Pooh of the time he had stamped in a puddle but instead of making its usual delicious, slop and slurp sound it had made a squeaky, cracking sound and Pooh had pulled out of the puddle a sharp slither of ice that glinted in the sun in an exciting, dangerous sort of way.

This tree, if it really was a tree, also looked exciting and dangerous but very beautiful and if Pooh leaned back as far as he could go without toppling over he could just see the point at the top disappearing into the clouds.

The next stop for the bus was near the River Thames and the friends walked along until they came to a bridge.

It was quite the longest bridge they had ever been on and they began to wonder if there really was another side when they saw the dome of St Paul's Cathedral rise up in front of them.

Pooh and Piglet stopped for a little rest in the middle and did what anyone sensible would do on such a fine bridge – played Poohsticks. But it wasn't a great success.

Pooh was certain that his stick had won and Piglet argued that they were the wrong type of sticks and had sunk. In any case, the truth was that the river was so far down that they couldn't see their sticks at all and so they had to content themselves with waving at the passengers on the boats beneath them and that was a very cheering thing to do.

The bus tour continued to Trafalgar Square.

'Look out for the lions,' said the driver.

'Lions!' gasped Piglet in some alarm. And there were indeed lions but thankfully not the furry ones with hot breath and hungry eyes that they were imagining. These lions were cold and majestic and their backs were shiny from where many people had sat upon them.

'Oh, how I'd love to have a lion,' Christopher Robin sighed. But Pooh thought that bears were best and pulled Christopher Robin back to the bus.

The tour then took them past an enormous clock in a high up tower. Christopher Robin told them that this clock's largest bell was called Big Ben.

'I feel sure,' said Pooh, 'that with this clock I could really learn to tell the time. With smaller clocks I do try to tell it, but it just doesn't listen; the numbers jump about so and o'clock isn't an O at all and seconds aren't a little something more to eat and everything gets so terribly muddled. A clock like this though, is sure to behave itself.'

But just then, a sudden gust of wind pulled the balloon up and away. It looked so wonderful flying next to Big Ben that Piglet couldn't feel sad and, in any case, he was too excited because the next stop was Buckingham Palace.

'Oh Pooh,' whispered Piglet, as they climbed off the bus, 'isn't it grand.'

And it certainly was. Behind golden gates, windows rose up in every direction. Rows and rows of windows and above it all the Royal Standard flag waved proudly in the sky.

'The flag means that the Queen is at home,' announced Christopher Robin who knew a great deal about Queens and such like because he had come to Buckingham Palace once before, many years ago.

'Well, it's all very well for some,' complained Eeyore. 'I've never had a flag myself. But then, I'm always at home. One boggy place is much like another and I don't hold with all this packing up and Farewell and See You Soon palaver.'

At that moment a bugle sounded. Piglet gave a startled jump and then continued jumping in time with the marching band to show that it hadn't been a startled jump at all. The Queen's Guard marched past. They were splendid in their bright red uniforms, shiny buttons and tall furry hats.

'What do you think they keep under their hats, Pooh?' asked Piglet, a little out of breath after all his jumping.

'Perhaps a little something to nibble on ... Just a smackerel of something ... sticky perhaps ... sweet certainly ...' Pooh's voice faded off into a happy dream.

But all at once, there was a stirring in the crowd and the murmur rose up, 'It's the Queen. The Queen is coming.'

Pooh and Piglet squeezed their way to the front of the crowd.

And then they saw a sight that they had always secretly hoped for but had never dared imagine might really happen. The Queen herself was out for a stroll and she was greeting the crowd as she went. She was just as Queenly and smiley and wonderful as they had expected her to be.

The Queen was so close that they could have reached out and touched her fine coat. Winnie-the-Pooh knew that it was now or never. Boldly he stepped forward and recited his hum in the loudest, bravest voice he could manage in the circumstances. The Queen smiled warmly at them all.

'Where's Eeyore?' asked Christopher Robin anxiously, as the Queen walked on to greet other people in the crowd. With all the excitement they had quite forgotten about him and then they saw him with his back to them, staring up at the palace.

'I believe I saw the Queen at one of the windows,' he announced proudly.

'But Eeyore ...' began Piglet, 'the Queen just ...'

'We must be heading home now,' interrupted Christopher Robin, who couldn't bear to disappoint dear old Eeyore, who had missed the whole thing.

Later, when the story had been retold over and over again, Winnie-the-Pooh was sure that the Queen had said, 'How charming.' But what was certain was that the hum had been shared and the Queen had gone. She was back behind the tall, golden gates of Buckingham Palace where no bear could go.

'Do you think the Queen liked my hum, Christopher Robin?' asked Pooh as they walked down The Mall.

'Silly Old Bear, I'm sure of it,' he replied, squeezing his paw a little tighter.

'London is a very fine place,' announced Pooh, but he was very tired and happy to be on his way back home, where a little smackerel of something was sure to be awaiting them.

What Winnie-the-Pooh didn't realise was that his very first home was in fact in London, in that grand shop that he had passed on the bus. He also didn't know that he had arrived in the Forest in the very same year that Princess Elizabeth was born. But time is a tricky thing; years begin by lazing along slowly and then suddenly, up they jump and off they trot as quickly as ever they can. To Winnie-the-Pooh, it felt like just yesterday that he had come bumping down those stairs. Bump, bump, bump.

And that is just the way it should be.

Winnie-the-Pooh

Colourful and collectible editions of
A.A.Milne's much-loved classic books.

Available in all good bookshops and online.

www.egmont.co.uk

Give the gift of a personalised book

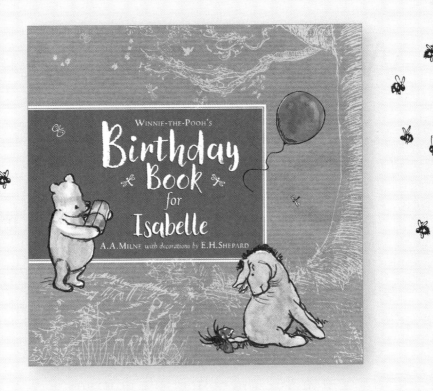

For our full range of books, perfect for every occasion,
visit **shop.egmont.co.uk**